Dance of

fireflies

Taming The Impostor Saga Book i

Adventure Time Travel Fantasy Series

Sheri Vie

Doctor Vie Publications

Discover More

Learn about the African setting for the series.
www.DrVie.com/Taming-The-Impostor-map

A Gift For You

Prequel to Taming The Impostor Saga
Utopian Planet Zooka
www.DrVie.com/VIPfreebooks

Dance Of Fireflies Dedication

Honors my dearest Mom, who supports and accompanies me
on many of the "back-routes" featured in Taming the
Impostor Saga.

And in reverence to
the memory of my dearest Dad, who piqued my love for
adventure, which catalyzed the characters.

And to
the memory of my dearest Grandma, and her fascinating
stories of superpowers and Utopian legends, sprinkled
throughout the Saga.

And recently
in memory of my dear friend Michael-Sean O'Connell, passed
at age 29 on 7 January 2017, who at my side in 2016,
encountered a young boy in South Africa, who inspired the
character of Siya.

CONTENTS

CHAPTER ONE

Royal Utopian Family Bonds

J ALI SKIPPED AND HOPPED, and his arms swung fast as he struggled to keep up with Reena's pace across the Royal Garden.

"What is going on? Why this rapid sequence of events? Why not go after the birthday celebration?"

The Zookian princess ground to a halt and with the strength of a hundred warriors she pierced her newly acquired Spear of Vee into the sand. Through the settling dust, her Third Eye drew her brother to the red bush hedge, as she stared down at him.

"Jali, I know what you are thinking. Remember what Grandma said? Time is at stake."

He fidgeted and moped.

She tilted his hot face up toward her. "Before you know it, I will return for your Level-4 graduation. You must attend to your lessons with Guardian 1. Surprise me with the new applications. I know you have been working on them." Reena pulled him close and tousled his tuft of unruly hair. "Promise?"

Unable to shake the uneasiness deep in his stomach, the little prince buried his face in his hands.

"Jee, listen, I miss Mama and Papa, too." She pried away his damp hands, and her face grew sad. "We cannot turn back time. We cannot bring them back."

"But I want to be strong and protect you and Grandma. I want to protect all of Zooka." And try as might, his attempt to control his emotions failed, as his chest heaved, his breathing quickened, and his skin flushed.

Reena reached for him, and a familiar calmness rushed through his body; lowering his heartbeat and cooling his skin.

"The reason you were unable to light the birthday candles was because you did not focus on the present moment."

"Reena!" He tightened his eyebrows and stared into her large green eyes. "But, *you* lit the candles!"

She shrugged and appeared unperturbed. "I helped you, but no one noticed. That is a sister's role. We are one, you and I."

"Ooka, Reena we are one." He hugged her. A soft tremor rippled through his body, and he held back tears.

"Oh, I love you too, little Jee." She kissed his head before changing her tone. "Now, about Tuttles." Her eyebrow lifted, the way it always did when she unraveled his secrets.

Her Third Eye opened.

Jali's gaze darted from left to right, unable to avoid the emerald glare. *"Oh dear, you know."*

"Ooka, I know."

Letting out a short snort, he turned and signaled to the bush. There was not much he could hide from Reena's well-trained Third Eye. She could see almost everything!

"Come out, Tuttles. She knows!"

Flying out from the bushes and over the greenery Tuttles emerged, and landed with a thump at her feet.

"Glad to meet you, Tuttles. You take care of my little brother, understood?"

She patted the green humped shell of the four-legged reptilian as he smiled, blinked his massive eyes, and dipped his thick neck into the shell house.

"Jali, you are in charge while I am away. Take care of Grandma, the Royal Garden, and our life forms. I know you will be at the summit, watching Zooble beam off. I wish you would not be so scared each time I leave."

The Magnificent ZW7 landed behind the hedge and tears threatened again.

"Time to go, little Jee. Remember everything we

discussed?"

He nodded.

"I shall communicate with you through the Zookian Glass." Reena poised her strong, limber body for action.

Retrieving the Spear of Vee, she raised it, and flew over the hedge.

Princess Reena and the Magnificent ZW7 took off toward the Zooble Dome.

❋ ❋ ❋ ❋ ❋ ❋

CHAPTER TWO

A Prince's Challenge

LETTING OUT A DEEP sigh Jali turned to his trusted friend. "Our secret is still safe."

The creature's blue tongue darted. "You are correct, Your Highness. What is next on the agenda?"

Jali hoisted himself onto the firm shell. His Third Eye fluttered, and the pair became invisible.

Bending low he whispered, "Let us investigate."

Under their cloak of invisibility they flew over the garden, approached the Royal Cave, and floated through the open window.

Protector 1 and Queen Vraka were sharing thought waves. Jali tugged at his ear; he wished he would graduate out of Level-4 and access the Zookian superpowers of mind-reading.

His pointed ears perked when the pair returned to

Zookish and his super-hearing tuned in.

"We must meditate for the Princess's success on this mission," Protector 1 advised Queen Vraka. "If she fails, many civilizations and much more will perish."

They faded into telepathy.

Jali flinched, before his ears perked again, and to his delight they continued in Zookish.

"It is a pity that Prince Jali has not graduated to Level-5. He could be a strong asset by observing the Princess on Zooble."

Jali's heart lurched, and he struggled to maintain his attention.

Queen Vraka chuckled. "He certainly takes after his father. I recall his struggle with Level-4, too." Her voice softened. "His legacy is a source of pride for this planet."

Protector 1 agreed. "Come, my Queen, I have prepared the Zookian Glass." He bowed and followed her. "Now, tell me, does Princess Reena have the secret mission guides for when she...?"

They switched to telepathy and exited the Royal Counsel Chamber.

Cut off from the conversation, Jali puffed and tugged at his ears. Wiping the bothersome tears off his face, he slid off the green hump.

"Did you hear that, Tuttles? *If* I learned faster and graduated in time off Level-4, I *could* be stronger; I *would* be keeping everyone safe. I *would* be on Zooble observing the mission. But I am *not*!"

With his hands behind his back, he paced on the stony floor. "Reena is leaving me once again." He flicked a burgeoning teardrop off his nose. "I *wish* I could turn back the clock so Mama and Papa would never have left on that dreadful mission." Feeling abandoned he sank to his knees and sobbed.

The reptile flicked his blue tongue on the prince's wet face. "Crying serves no purpose, Your Highness."

Jali pondered on his wise friend's words, and his mind galloped as he widened his eyes and grinned. "I may have a purposeful plan."

❋ ❋ ❋ ❋ ❋ ❋

CHAPTER THREE

Intergalactic Space Explorer

IN THE ROYAL OBSERVATION CHAMBER, Queen Vraka floated with her Lotus Wand. On the Zooble Dome below, the Magnificent ZW7 followed Reena into the Zooble intergalactic space explorer.

Inside the tubular craft, one hundred Zookian warriors prepared the bubble for their expedition, and as the Magnificent ZW7 set Zooble for intergalactic travel, Commander ZW1 and Reena waved to the gathering cheering outside. Within a blip, the Peace-Keeping Force zoomed past millions of stars to the edge of Galaxy Thare, and planet Zooka disappeared into a void.

Reena wished her brother would not hide each time she left on a mission. The image of Jali tugging at her feet before she boarded Zooble on her first journey flashed before her, and her stomach knotted. He had run away from the Royal Observation Chamber and hid in their favorite viewpoint at the summit to secretly watch the takeoff. Today she was sure he would be watching her from his hideout.

She sighed, turning her attention to the activity around her in the Control Chamber at the anterior of the explorer. The legendary reputation of Commander ZW1, Chief of the Peace-Keeping Force, was revered throughout the Cosmos. And as she had done so many times before, she marveled at him orchestrating their Zarp-speed through the galaxies. But today was different. She was interning as their supervisor, and she would soon have to prove herself.

"Princess Reena, the periphery of Galaxy Al86 approaches," Commander ZW1 said.

Their Z-Clock displayed 13:00:00

She lowered her gaze and opened her Third Eye to project the deep blue Zookian Glass, their communication mode.

Within, Protector 1 and Queen Vraka appeared. "Esteemed Commander ZW1, when Zooble crosses over and traverses through Cosmo 13 there is no returning until your mission is accomplished. You have ninety Z-days to find planet Earth, locate the SOS, discover the deviancy, and restore precisely what has altered."

"Understood, Queen Vraka," Commander ZW1 said.

"Zookian wishes to you, Zooble, planet Earth, and

my dear Princess. The coordinates to enter the Portal avail." Queen Vraka raised her Lotus Wand and faded away.

Reena's heart palpitated. They were not only bound by the crucial time deadline, but also by their inexperience; none of them had previously journeyed through the newly disclosed Portal.

Commander ZW1 clicked his heels. "Princess Reena, we await your supervision to cross over."

She composed her racing heart and followed him to the iridescent Zookian Locator in their loyal Transporter.

For years, Reena had watched her mentor initiate crossings into many dimensions. Now that her time had arrived, she wavered, but Commander ZW1 spurred her on. Inhaling deeply and, with caution, the princess streamed the coordinates through her Third Eye, and as she released her breath, triggered the sequence.

Darkness blanketed the Control Chamber, spreading a vacuum of silence around her; evaporating her body.

Nothingness.

Endless.

Nothingness.

"Reena, I am scared!"

"Do not worry, Jali, I am safe."

"Please do not leave me, Reena. Come back, Reena. Come back."

"I am not leaving you, Jee. I will never leave you behind."

* * * * * *

CHAPTER FOUR

Crossing Over

A FAMILIAR HUM RESOUNDED around Reena, and a cool breeze brushed against her cheek. She drew in a short breath.

The Z-Clock flashed 14:00:00.

At the helm, Commander ZW1 supervised Zooble's expedition through waves of expected turbulence as they ventured through Cosmo 13.

The expanding warmth in Reena's arms caught her attention. She gasped.

"Jali, you should not be here. Jee, what have you done?" Instinctively she embraced her brother.

He looked wide-eyed, speechless; his body was over-heating. She tightened her grip on him, and with her Third Eye permeated cool energy through his little body, stabilizing his thermo regulator. Like a mother, she rocked him as he rejuvenated and smiled at her. "Oh,

Jali."

"Princess Reena, Queen Vraka and Protector 1 await at the Zookian Glass." Commander ZW1 startled at Jali's presence, and steadied the prince before they reported on their progress.

"Your Highness, we have successfully entered Cosmo 13. Vitals on Zooble register one hundred percent. Princess Reena, Prince Jali, and Tuttles are safe," Commander ZW1 said.

"Pardon?"

"Ooka, Grandma, Jali and Tuttles are on board," Reena explained.

From behind her, Jali edged closer, in full view of the Zookian Glass.

"Little one, why did you sneak on Zooble?" Queen Vraka asked.

✳ ✳ ✳ ✳ ✳ ✳

CHAPTER FIVE

Growing Pains

Jali SQUIRMED, TAKING IN quick short breaths. "I am old enough, Grandma. Reena left on her first mission when she turned fourteen!"

He nodded vigorously and pursed his lips, ignoring the stunned Magnificent ZW7 warriors. Reena and Commander ZW1 stared at him, their Third Eyes fluttering fast.

Grandma and Protector 1 shared telepathic thoughts and shook their heads.

"What is wrong?" Jali turned to Reena.

"I did not want to tell you in this manner, Jee." She placed her hands on his shoulders. "Before Mama and Papa left on their final mission, they instructed Zooka to protect you until you turn thirty. You are vulnerable until then."

"Grandma, I do not understand. Why am I different?

What is wrong with me? I am strong. I can do almost everything Reena did when she went on her first mission. It is not fair. I want to grow up too!"

He sniffed and sped out of the Control Chamber with his devoted friend Tuttles at his side.

✳ ✳ ✳ ✳ ✳ ✳

CHAPTER SIX

Royal Confidence Boost

ON THEIR WAY OUT of the Control Chamber, Tuttles and Jali startled a Zookian warrior.

"What are you doing here, Prince Jali? You should not be here."

Nobody wants me around!

The young prince brushed past the warrior, and ran through the narrow passageway, recalling Reena's description of the Royal Zooble Chamber. Barging in, he sank onto the leafy bed, with Tuttles hovering beside him.

"Tuttles, why do they treat me like a little child?"

"Adulthood is at age thirty, Your Highness."

"You know what I mean. I am fourteen and I qualify for my first mission. Besides, I have been mastering my secret superpowers."

Within moments, Reena joined them, her protective

Force-1 Shield glowed bright. "I know you want to protect Grandma, Zooka and me. But you must be patient, little brother."

"What is wrong with me?"

"There is nothing wrong with you. Today you overcame your fear of exploring Zooble."

He smiled, feeling light and empowered.

"But your courage has placed the rescue mission at risk. We cannot return to Zooka until we rescue the threatened beings." She frowned with apparent concern. "You are protected from harm if you remain on Zooka or within Zookian protection."

Jali ignored her troubled words, and his voice squeaked with excitement. "You think I was brave, Reena?" He winked at Tuttles.

She eyed him with suspicion.

Raising himself on tiptoes, he unveiled his proposal. "I have an idea. I can stay protected on board Zooble and complete my internship with Guardian 1 through the Zookian Glass, while you are on your ground rescue mission, on planet Earth."

Her Third Eye scanned him for signs of mischief, but he had none. "Agreed. You observe me from Zooble and gain mastery of your Level-4 skills."

He grinned. "Agreed."

"Now tell me, how did you hide from my scanner?"

"Oh, no!"

"Ooka, out with it now!"

"There was an anomaly when I applied Level-4 powers to help me fly, making Tuttles and me invisible."

"For what length of time are you two undetectable?"

He shrugged. "I cannot predict, it varies."

To his relief, Commander ZW1's voiced disturbed her line of questioning. "Princess Reena, you are wanted in the Control Chamber."

She turned to Jali. "Very well. We shall revisit this later." Opening her Third Eye, she transmitted an announcement through the space explorer. "Zookian warriors, Prince Jali will remain on Zooble, complete his Level-4 practice, and observe our mission through the Zookian Glass. You are to protect him, and regulate his thermo fluctuations as needed."

Jali chortled and winked at Tuttles.

"Princess Reena, you are wanted in the Control Chamber," Commander ZW1 repeated.

Fortified with his new agenda, Jali's confidence rose. *I can complete Level-4 and observe Reena!*

He bounced in step with her on their way to the Control Chamber.

The little prince smiled His adventures had finally begun.

❋ ❋ ❋ ❋ ❋ ❋

CHAPTER SEVEN

Beaming To Planet Earth

"PRINCESS, WE ARE APPROACHING Andromeda Galaxy," Commander ZW1 reported as they entered the Control Chamber.

Now that he could freely observe their journey, instead of hiding in the chef's pantry, the fascinating view of the galaxies, suns and planets from their translucent craft, enthralled Jali.

"Milky Way," Commander ZW1 announced.

"Solar System."

"That is planet Earth," he said, pointing straight ahead.

Jali gasped with delight.

"Engage P1 invisible shield," Reena instructed the team as Zooble circled the little land-filled planet. "Locate the source of the SOS and derive intelligence about the beings and activities of the planet."

A Magnificent ZW7 warrior conveyed the data, "Humans dominate, but ninety percent of their kind function at Level-1. The SOS emanated from the large landmass named Africa."

Commander ZW1 confirmed the location. "We are zooming in to southern Africa, to the tip named South Africa, in a region of KwaZulu-Natal, to an area of habitation, Chatsworth. The SOS left Chatsworth twenty-four Earth hours past."

Around them the Control Chamber whirred with activity, and Reena turned to Jali. "Jee, remember your promise. You need to remain secure."

Agreeing, he followed her to the Transporter.

"Princess Reena, we transport in sixty Z-seconds," Commander ZW1 announced.

"Acknowledged," she said, and joined him.

Tuttles hovered near Jali as Reena, Commander ZW1, and the Magnificent ZW7 positioned themselves in the hollow Transporter, and opened their Third Eyes. Rings of white lights circled them, before the launch team began the countdown sequence.

10...9...8...7...6...5...4...3...2...1...0.

Jali's pulse quickened, his ears perked, and his Third Eye fluttered.

Something is wrong!

An eruption clamped his ears shut. He fell to his

knees and shielded his eyes from the vivid red hue and waves of vibration as the Transporter splintered. His heart raced.

"We are disintegrating, stop the sequence!" Reena shouted.

"The interference is too resilient, we are unable to terminate!" the launch team shouted back.

Jali cried and ran to the tunneling hole in the Transporter, in which the ZW7 warriors had already fallen. "Reena!"

She was fading fast; dropping farther into the terrifying dark pit.

He flattened himself onto the shuddering floor and stretched as far as he could. "Reena, hold on to my hand!"

But her fingers drifted farther from him, and her large green eyes pleaded, as she, Commander ZW1, and the Magnificent ZW7 began to vaporize.

Jali could feel Tuttles' grip on his ankles, as he leaned even lower into the gaping hole, and shouted. "Reenaaaaaa!"

✳ ✳ ✳ ✳ ✳ ✳

CHAPTER EIGHT

Mystery Adventure

"BIRTHDAY CAKE!"

Youngsters laughed, giggled, and shrieked with delight amid a scent of fresh roses. The familiar sounds and smells embraced Jali as he opened his eyes, and felt even more comforted by purple swallows, flying high above in the clear blue atmosphere.

I must have dozed off.

Brushing smidgens of grass off his legs, he arose from the bush, and stretched his arms above his ears. A twang of pain shot through his head. He cringed, squeezed his eyes, and let out a mournful groan.

Brela... I wonder where she is?

Tall trees lined a stony narrow path and wound down to the source of the laughter. His ears perked.

They could not have started without me!

Pushing his way through thick shrubs, he followed the winding trail of mirth, on the lookout for Brela's bushy tail.

In the clearing ahead of him, a dark-skinned boy about his height, the top of his braided black hair covered with leaves, peered into the edge of a window set in an odd-shaped brown cave. Balanced on a rock, the boy held a smooth stick in one hand and a stack of identically sized white leaves in the other.

"Careful, you're ruining my Halloween cape." A girl's voice flowed out of the cave.

"Okay, settle down. Now that you have your slices of cake, back to the lesson," an older female voice from inside the cave added.

A twig snapped under Jali's feet as he neared the boy, who looked startled and shook his head with annoyance. Jali froze and watched with curiosity as the boy pushed a double glass object on his nose.

"Shhh," the boy whispered and flapped his hand downward. "Get down." He returned to spying on the cave. "Do you want us to get caught?"

Jali dropped to his knees, crawled to reach the boy, and studied him. *What an odd life form.*

From inside the cave, the older female voice asked, "What is the 143 element?"

"Bulnitramet," the boy whispered.

"Shiana, what on earth are you up to again?" the older female said.

"N-nothing, M-Miss Amber," a girl replied.

Children's laughter rang out.

"That's enough!" Miss Amber said. "The answer is Bulnitramet BLM, and since none of you know this, your homework is to memorize the chemistry table before your next lab session."

The children moaned.

"Yes, that's enough time after your Halloween party."

A jarring noise shattered the air. Jali flinched, his ears snapped shut and he crouched into a ball-shape near the boy, who stared at him.

"Hayibo, that's not the police." He patted Jali's head. "Silly, it's just the school siren!"

The boy slapped Jali's knee. "Come on, let's go before they see us!" He turned, sped past Jali, and disappeared over a shrub hedge; the tuft of leaves from his head flying into the air.

Behind them, the chatter of children softened as Jali followed, jumped over the bush, and into a garden. He paused to rest his hands on his knees and catch his breath. He could feel the sweat streaming down his face, and he rubbed his neck.

I am becoming hot! Where is everyone?

"Have you seen Brela?" he asked the curly haired boy.

It was their first eye-to-eye contact. The boy jumped backward, his eyes widened, and he dropped the white-leaved papyrus and stick from his hands. Fixing his gaze on Jali he slowly bent to pick up the leaves. He relaxed, smiled, and shrugged. "Aikona, not sure who that is." His eyes brightened. "Hey, are you having a jol for Halloween?" He pointed to Jali's Third Eye, ears, and clothing.

"Halloween? Jol?"

The boy narrowed his gaze. "Yebo." He sighed and appeared sad, before lowering his head. He looked up, squinted, and scanned Jali's face. The boy's large black eyes widened again and stepping back toward the tree, he tilted his head. "Hey, are you from the US or are you with the Dragons?"

"US? Dragons?" Jali repeated, his face hotter than ever.

In the silence, they eyed each other from head to toe. The boy smacked his full lips, inspected him with curiosity and said, "You stole the outfit, didn't you?" He walked around Jali scrutinizing him. "You don't look like one of them." He pushed the strange glass at the tip of his nose back on his face. "Don't worry, I won't tell."

Sweat drenched Jali's back, and drops from his

sweltering forehead bothered his vision. Blinking fast he watched the boy with absorption, until his super-hearing perked, and his gaze darted left.

The boy jerked his head in the direction of the loud screams. "Aikona, no! The Dragons are here. Come on, let's go."

He tugged at Jali's arm and ran ahead.

Jali sped behind the boy. The screams grew louder as they approached a fence of shrubs and molded themselves snugly into the foliage. He wrinkled his nose. *What is that awful odor?*

Over the hedge, on a rubble-path, two warriors clothed in long, dark coats shoved a group of youngsters into a large-wheeled, shuttle-like vehicle. In the front sat a fair-skinned younger man.

He looked out of the window and yelled. "Come on, that's enough captives for today."

The tall warrior kicked a boy. A girl captive ran to help him, her faced discolored with tears. Both warriors rebuked her and flung the two into the shuttle.

A rancid odor plumed from the vehicle, and Jali coughed.

"Hey!" the shorter warrior shouted. "There's someone in the bushes."

"Let's get him!"

Next to Jali, the boy yelled. "Run!" But he tripped on

a boulder, and Jali bent to help him.

From the bushes behind them, the warriors jumped. Jali whirled with shock; flared his nostrils, and stood tall. "What Zookian level are you at?" He cocked his head to one side and demanded an answer for their wayward behavior.

The warriors roared with laughter.

His eyes narrowed. They did not look like any warriors he had seen before. Where are their Third Eyes? They were not Zookian warriors. The boy also did not have a Third Eye!

The taller man dashed past to the boy whilst the second assailant rushed close to him and even closer as he stepped back.

The man's red eyes glinted and he smirked. "Hello, hello, hello, what do we have here?"

Spit splattered on Jali. Stunned, he wiped his hot face and confronted the bully. "I command you to stop at once!" he said, raising his voice.

The man scoffed. "Another freak for Halloween." He turned and looked at the boy. "Bring that freaky, four-eyed know-it-all here," he said.

The tall man lunged at the boy and dragged him close. "Siya, I see you found yourself a buddy, ja?" He jabbed a finger into Jali's chest and beamed.

Jali's heart lurched.

The boy named Siya, pushed the glass onto his face, straightened his shoulders, and nodded. "Yebo, he's my friend." He turned his head to one side, appearing confident. "Yebo, from the US and we're going to a jol. But we didn't see anything."

The attacker chuckled. "I think today's the day for a detour!" He shoved the papyrus from Siya's hand and tramped on it.

The boy dropped to his knees, his hands to his head, and he groaned. "Noooo..." The strange glass object fell off his nose, landing beside him.

In a flash the attacker stomped on it, crushing it to smithereens.

The boy sobbed hysterically.

Jali scuttled to his aid and glared at the men. "Stop all your unworthy actions. You are hurting Siya!"

He helped the boy off his knees, picked up the torn pieces of papyrus, and stared up into the men's fiery eyes.

The dark-haired man, quick as lightning, swung back his right fist. Unbearable pain ripped through Jali's abdomen and the garden spun and blurred. He screamed and crashed into the bushes, blinking fast. Someone rushed to him. Jolts of pain shot through his left side, his right side, and again on his left side. He moaned as he used his hands to block the attacker.

The man laughed, his hot breath on his face "That

will serve you right, you freak from the US. Right, ha ha!"

From behind them, children's laughter neared, severing the heightened tension.

"School's out. That's enough now, Dragons. Let's get out of here. They're waiting to process the captives," their leader shouted from across the hedge, and their footsteps vanished into the rustle of bushes.

Jali's body throbbed with unfamiliar soreness as the garden gradually stopped spinning.

A soft hand cradled his head, and a scent of roses flowed into his nostrils.

"Grandma, Reenaaa…"

❄ ❄ ❄ ❄ ❄ ❄

CHAPTER NINE

Visionary Pure Ones

A FRAGRANCE OF RED ROSES permeated the little backyard, cheered the cracked walls of the rumbling old house, and ignited a smile on Kriaka's chocolate-brown, heart-shaped face. She tilled the fertile soil around the flower garden, sprinkled drops of water she had saved all through the week onto the thirsty leaves, and softly sang.

"We shall overcome some day, hey, hey..."

A latch squeaked open at her side. Meosic jumped off the trapdoor, but not fast enough as loose patches of grass and sand tickled her whiskers. She stretched her neck and meowed in annoyance.

Rama's head of curly long black hair jutted over the flap. He winked his hazel-brown eye, propped his chiseled arms on either side of the outlet, heaving his tall body onto the grass, and joined Kriaka's song.

"Our sun glows bright
We dream of doves each night
Our voices will soon have their say, hey, hey.
Their say, hey, hey."

He bent to kiss her head, and patted her shoulders with his strong hands, as she instinctively wrinkled her nose.

"Smell of a hard-working bloke, sis." Rama chuckled and with one greasy hand, swiped his sweaty neck and puffed. "Man, is it hot down there!"

Kriaka offered him a rag and poured a short, hazy glass of water from the jug at her side.

Meosic rubbed her furry back on his legs, looked up at him, and meowed.

The summer sun shimmered over her brother's muscular body, showing off his biceps as he guzzled, reached for more, and gulped. He tilted his chin, and wiped his goatee and unshaven face on his faded T-shirt.

"Less than an hour and we should be set for tonight." After rubbing his hands with the old cloth, he took aim at her.

Like an agile dragonfly, she snatched the greasy rag, as he headed to the secret basement and pulled the wooden decoy over him.

With caution, she replaced the patch of grass over the trapdoor; enticing Meosic to resume her favorite spot for sunbathing.

What was that?

A strange shudder ran through Kriaka's body, and her heart missed a beat. She dusted her sandy fingers on the well-worn blue dress flowing around her small hips and wiped tiny beads of sweat off her forehead. Close to her feet, Meosic's tail stiffened, and the pair watched the hidden garden entrance in anticipation.

The bush parted; a small fair hand showed through.

"A-A-Akaaa," Shiana cried. The girl's slender form ran toward her, her Halloween wings tearing in the bush. "H-help him," she said, pointing behind her.

Siya appeared inside the secret garden with an unconscious little boy on his back; the boy's feet trailed on the grass. Meosic ran and tugged at his pants.

Kriaka rushed to Siya, as he collapsed with a huff and puff. They tried to catch the boy, before he fell; in vain.

With a bit of a struggle, she lifted the body and Siya rolled out from under.

"H-h-he's hurt. The Dragons beat him up," Shiana said.

"Okay, help me lift him inside," Kriaka whispered, her gaze darting around the garden.

Siya held the boy's legs, and they shuffled through the back door, placing him on the old couch in the corner of the sitting-room.

She drew the outmoded velvet curtains firmly across the windowpane. "Quick, bring water and some towels!"

The kids hurried to the kitchenette. Meosic brushed her tail against the boy and meowed.

"Who is he? What happened?"

The little girl hastened, spilling water from the bowl, her eyes as large as saucers. "H-heard crying. D-Dragons ran from the garden behind the school. I found S-S-Siya and the b-boy."

Kriaka moistened the tattered towels. "Siya? Who is he?"

"He maybe is from the US, but I dunno."

Puzzled, the two females stared at him.

Siya shrugged. "Ay, I saw him in the schoolyard, and then those Dragons got us." He touched the boy's hand. "Is he okay?"

Kriaka checked the boy's pulse. "He's too hot. Ana, go find Herb, he'll know what to do."

The girl rushed out the door.

Kriaka stood tall. "Siya, stay here, don't open the door, I'll get Rama."

He agreed, and Meosic curled close to the boy, licking his hands.

She smiled, bemused. That's a first—she must like the little stranger! Within seconds, she dashed out the back door and through the rose patch while monitoring the garden. Pulling open the wooden slab door, she glanced over her shoulder, and descended.

Rama's drilling, hammering, and cussing echoed as she walked down the cold tunnel toward the light. His head was bowed, intent on the engine.

She tapped his shoulder.

"Kriii! Careful."

She stared at him, speechless.

"What's wrong Kri? What's happened?"

"I'm not sure. Siya and Ana brought a little boy, beaten by the Dragons. He's unconscious and heating up. You'd better come check."

Her brother ran ahead of her into the house, where Siya and Meosic were magnetized by the little figure on the couch.

Rama frowned, and pulled Kriaka to the sink. "Who is he? Why is he here?"

"He's just a little boy."

"What if he's a spy? We can't risk it. There's too much to lose tonight!"

Meosic jumped onto the tiny fridge, stretched her

neck, and meowed at them.

Kriaka knit her eyebrows. Our cat is behaving strangely.

Rama walked to and fro, until she rested her hand on his chest.

"Look, why don't you finish the engine and check on the team. I'll see to the boy. I've a good feeling about him."

He appeared relieved; hugged her, and grabbing his cap and shades spoke in a hushed tone. "Tonight's our night! See you soon." The back door creaked shut behind him.

For a moment, Kriaka folded her arms and leaned against the squeaky wooden panel to catch her breath. Deep in thought, she readied the water to clean the boy's face. The gaudy novel cloth on his light-brown skin, was a Halloween trend for sure.

The dot between his eyes, did it change color? She sponged his face, careful not to cover it. His princely Halloween costume is fantastic, even the pointed ears. *I wonder where he's from.*

Siya seemed equally fascinated by the boy.

The kitchen door squeaked. Herby filled the doorway, huffing and puffing, with Shiana behind him. He kissed Kriaka's lips, knelt near the boy, and checked his pulse. Frowning, he touched the boy's face, shook his head, and frowned even more. He tried to open the boy's Halloween top but failed.

"He's temperature is rising. Get some more cold water."

Shiana ran back to the sink.

Kriaka's heart hammered. "He's changing color. His skin—it's turning green!"

The four exchanged glances.

Herby stared. "Where did you say he's from?"

Siya muttered. "Hayibo, I asked if he was from the US, and he didn't know about the US—didn't know Halloween, didn't know about jol!"

Kriaka beckoned Herby to the bedroom. "Stay here kids," she said and closed the shaky door.

"What do you think we are dealing with here, Kri?" Herby whispered, his eyes soft as he touched her face. "Does it have anything to do with the GIFT? I don't want anything to happen to you."

The back door scraped open. Footsteps drew closer and Rama entered, his voice full of excitement. "We're set. This is our last chance to find the GIFT. What time can we leave?"

Kriaka and Herby exchanged glances and shrugged. Herby indicated to the sitting-room.

Rama banged his fist into the wall. "Oh, no!" He wrenched off his cap and scratched his head. "Look, we leave him here, with Siya. When he's feeling better, Siya can take him to find his family."

✳ ✳ ✳ ✳ ✳ ✳

CHAPTER TEN

Third Eye Superpowers

FAMILY!

Jali inched his aching body around the soft couch. "Reena, Grandma?"

He tried to make sense of the dull ceiling that filled his visual field. Despite squeezing his eyes and opening them again, the ceiling remained muddy, and the damp odor offended his nostrils. He could not help but cough.

A movement at his side caught his attention; he narrowed his gaze. To his right sat the boy named Siya.

Alongside him stood a girl. Her shoulder-length golden hair hung loose around her fair face, her eyes deep blue, widened with fright. She blinked fast.

Neither of them had a Third Eye. *Their ears are not pointed.* His ears perked as he picked up on chatter.

"Where's Reena, where's Grandma?" His breathing

quickened, his clothing clung to his back, and he could feel beads of sweat spot his forehead. He tried to push himself up, but excruciating pain at his sides imprisoned him.

"Is that your mommy and granny? Don't worry, we'll find them," Siya said.

Jali broke into sobs. "Reena, Reena, Reena."

The boy clasped his hand, and the girl pressed his forehead with a wet cloth.

A cat jumped onto him. He rubbed its neck and pleaded, "Reena, call Reena." The cat's ear popped up around its broad brown face.

His own ears perked and straightened as Siya and the girl jumped back. The cat leaped off the bed and slid toward the location of the hum.

Bright blue light filled the small corner.

"Reena!" Jali squinted and wrenched himself up.

The two youngsters watched with their mouths wide open, next to them the cat stretched her neck and meowed.

The Zookian Glass emerged with Commander ZW1 and Reena, but their images were faint.

"Jali, I am safe and well," Reena said. "Listen. This transmission will end soon. You transported over to planet Earth. I cannot regulate your temperature. You must seek shelter in a cool cave as soon as possible if you are to survive. This is your prime concern right now. Understood?"

"Yes."

Reena looked at Siya and the girl who clutched him. "You must take my brother to a cool cave at once. Otherwise, he will disintegrate. Cool cave to reset his thermo..." The Zookian Glass faded.

Jali collapsed on the softness beneath him, and pushed the tufts of wet hair off his forehead. Reena was safe, but his temperature was the problem. Yes, of course, he needed a cave.

When he tried to speak, his mouth dried and his skin burned. Helplessly, he gave in and lay still.

The girl held on to Siya who sat close to him. "Ay, you're from another planet, ja?" Siya asked.

He nodded.

The boy gasped, his mouth opened wide. "The summer here is bad for you, ja?"

He nodded again.

"We must get you to the cave, ja?"

He nodded; his vision blurred.

Siya turned to the girl who was still rooted to the ground. "Shiana, we must do something or he'll die."

The cat meowed and rubbed its back on Jali. The boy pulled Shiana toward a door on the opposite side of the strange cave, opened it, and they disappeared. Jali's ears tuned in to the chatter.

Shiana spoke in an elevated voice. "Aka, y-you must b-believe us. The boy, Jali, is f-from another planet. His sister appeared in a hologram. R-R-Reeena. She spoke to us. He will die if we don't take him to a cool cave now."

"What nonsense is this, Shiana? You are imagining things," a man's gruff voice snapped.

Siya replied in a shrill voice. "No, Rama, I saw Reena too. She looked like the boy, Jali, but older. You know — that funny dot in the middle of the eyebrows and the pointed ears. Please, we must save him. We can't let him die."

"Siya could be right. I examined the boy. Never encountered anything like this before. He has a different body composition. His abnormal body color fits right in with what the kids are saying," a soothing male voice said. "Look, time is short not just for us, but for this boy, Jali, too. I can't let him die. We must decide. What do you think, Kri?"

A musical female voice replied, "The boy is exceptional. He's surely been sent to us for a reason. Perhaps us finding the GIFT could be linked to us helping him."

No one responded and she continued. "Once he's well, he can explain for himself. If we don't believe him, we don't have to do anything more."

"What about tonight? We must address the rebels," Rama said.

"I know a place," Siya said. "Near the meeting spot. Hey, lots of caves there. Yebo, you get nice and cold there now 'cos of—"

"Okay." Rama cut the boy off. "We must hurry."

The door opened.

A beautiful woman glowed in the doorway. Jali's heart missed a beat. Her long black hair curled around her brown face.

She noticed his glance and smiled. He relaxed and returned her smile. Behind her two men towered. A muscular bearded man with dark curly hair, and a slender blond man who wore a white coat.

Siya and Shiana weaved past them and dashed to Jali's side, while the cat curled up beside him and meowed.

He fixed his gaze on the woman.

She came to his side and sat close to him. A scent of roses caressed his nostrils. She looked deep into his eyes. He smiled as she clasped his right hand and placed her palm on his head.

"Welcome to our planet Earth. I'm Kriaka Adi," she said in a musical voice, and turned her head. "The little girl is my sister, Shiana, Ana, and the bearded man is my brother, Rama Adi. The one beside him attended to you.

He is my fiancé, Dr. Herby—Herb. Of course, Meosic is curled up at your feet. And I think you already met Siya."

She turned to Jali, and her hazel-brown eyes sparkled.

"What is your name, young one?"

He felt sheltered.

"I am called Prince Jali." He smiled before everything turned black.

✿ ✿ ✿ ✿ ✿ ✿

CHAPTER ELEVEN

Survival of the Fittest

K RIAKA PANICKED. *OH no!*
Herby rushed to the boy and felt his pulse. "He's passed out again." He touched the prince's forehead. "He sure is hot."

"Quick, there's no time to lose," she urged.

Rama prepared their transport, and Siya helped Herby with the prince. She and Shiana hurriedly packed for their precarious trip as they ran around the little shack in Arena Park, in the middle of Chatsworth, in the heart of South Africa.

Within minutes, Herby carried the boy over his shoulder, past the back door held open by Siya, and into Rama's faithful eight-seater truck. He laid the prince in the last row, and Meosic promptly curled at his feet.

Fast and quietly the troop piled into the bakkie. From

her passenger seat, Kriaka checked on Shiana in the row behind her, and returned Herby's loving smile. Rama revved faithful Jen, patted the dashboard, and set her in motion through the back garden. Siya yanked shut the hedge gate and hopped in beside Shiana. Solemnly, they drove northwest.

"What time do you expect the First Ones to gather in Giant's Castle?" Kriaka asked her brother.

She could sense his frustration as he adjusted his cap. "We sent the word for them to meet at nine p.m. The park will be deserted well before then." Rama looked at the dusty clock. "We should be there around eight p.m."

"Siya, how do we get to the cave from the park?" Kriaka asked.

"I'll know the way when we get to the park."

Meosic jumped and curled up on Shiana's lap.

Kriaka winked at Herby, who as usual grasped the chance to pucker his lips and blow her a kiss. "Siya, we'll have to leave you with Prince Jali in the cave and head to the meeting arena. We'll swing by afterwards. You'll be okay?"

"Yebo, I know that place inside out. It's cool, and he'll get better there."

The little lost green-eyed boy tugged at Kriaka's heart. His body appeared weakened from the foreign surroundings, and his skin had become greener when

Herby laid him on the seat.

Tonight was important. They had to remain focused on the meeting with the First Ones and galvanize their plan to hunt for the GIFT. She placed her hand on Rama's, and sighed. Now they had one more variable to consider.

Even though a crease deepened on his forehead, she felt an odd sensation of relief, as she rubbed his shoulder. But he stared straight ahead.

They jolted through the back roads as loyal Jen chugged them along the five-hour trip toward the nature reserve.

In the distance, an impending storm threatened the afternoon sky.

❄ ❄ ❄ ❄ ❄ ❄

After several hours on the untarred roads surrounded by sparse vegetation, undetected by the Dragons, they passed the once inhabited town of Mooi River and entered a treacherous unmarked route.

A bolt of lightning whipped Kriaka and the worried troop in the bakkie to attention.

Siya counted. "1...2...3...4...5..." and at the roar of thunder, Shiana shrieked.

"The lightning struck one point six kilometers away," he said, with a wise grin on his face.

The sky opened like a burst dam, and a torrent of rain pelted Jen's tin roof. Rama maneuvered her between deep puddles in the section notorious for potholes. They'd purposely chosen the back route, a stretch of red sand and stones, which discouraged regular traffic. A nightmare on any good day, the dirt road now worsened with the torrential downpour.

Except for the bounce of Jen's booster headlights, the path remained invisible.

"Glad I installed the headlamps yesterday," Rama shouted, above the clatter of rain.

Kriaka strained her neck. The pitch-black at the rear of the truck and the incessant roar of rain drowned any hope for conversation.

Without warning they hurled from their seats so hard that Meosic hit the ceiling with a horrendous shriek—or was that Shiana? And they fell like a roller coaster on its steep descent.

Jen did not move. Rama crashed his fist into the cracked dashboard, cussed, then spoke in a somewhat restrained voice. "Is everyone all right back there?"

Kriaka could feel his irritation.

Soft squeaks flowed to the front. "Yeah, we're okay," Shiana and Siya replied.

"Ja, okay," Herby said.

Rama switched on the flashlight, pulled his cap off

his head, and wiped his forehead with the back of his hand. "This is all we need right now," he said and groaned.

After replacing his cap, he pulled the worn-out hoodie over his head, kicked open the door, and jumped out.

Siya shoved open the back door and joined him, and within seconds, poked his dripping wet head through Kriaka's window. "Jen's in a big donga! Ay, we have to carry her out!"

She tightened her hood, and ramming open the rusty door, stepped into a cold, mucky hole. Behind her, Herby guided Shiana. The storm cut out any communication whilst they trudged with Rama around Jen. He directed them to push from the back then returned to the truck and revved her. At his signal, the foursome forced with all their might.

Jen screeched but did not budge. Rama signaled again. They tried, but she remained glued in the ditch. Shiana screamed and slipped. Kriaka pulled the collar of the little girl's jacket before Rama gave the sign once more. They thrust their soggy bodies against Jen, but she was in too deep, and they relinquished.

It was useless.

What next?

Out of the haziness, headlights reflected on the Jen's

bumper. She jerked, lit up, and easily skidded out of the ditch.

Kriaka's body trembled. She turned and instinctively shielded her eyes, quickly pulling Shiana close. Rama slammed the door and joined them.

Someone emerged from the vehicle and stomped toward the group. Kriaka felt Herby's protecting hand on her shoulder, yet her mind raced as a large silhouette in a long coat and hood emerged through the headlights.

Its authoritative voice boomed above the noise of the pouring rain. "Are you okay?"

"Yeah!" Rama shouted, his voice laden with suspicion.

They watched the vague outline of the man, as Rama continued. "We just hit a spot of trouble, but it seems okay now."

"I'm Pierre—are you the First Ones' leader?"

Rama stepped forward and bade the troop get in the truck. The young ones obeyed, but Herby stood even closer to Kriaka.

She did not move, her gaze fixed on Pierre. "Who are you?"

He came nearer. She felt Herby's grip tighten on her shoulders, as Rama positioned himself between the man and her.

"Chill out, my bru," Pierre drawled. "I'm one of your

attendees. Lookin' forward to the meet."

Rama remained silent.

The stranger's loud voice seemed close to Kriaka's ears. "Look, my fog lamps are real strong. Whaddaya say I go ahead and you lot follow me—easy enough to do. We're not too far off now."

Rama hesitated. After a few seconds, he muttered. "Yeah, we can follow you up to the entrance. We need to fill petrol there, then we'll meet you up at the hall."

"Okay, see you at the entrance to the park." Pierre stared straight at Kriaka. "It's my pleasure to meet you." The man dipped his head, and walked backward. He spun around, and vanished into his vehicle.

The trio heaved their soaked bodies into the truck.

Rama started Jen in one go. "Thank goodness, I thought no one else knew this back road."

Kriaka checked the back. The kids and Meosic seemed settled. "How's Prince Jali?" she asked Herby.

He shone the torch at the boy. "The storm and drop in temperature are helping him, and I think he is less green now." His tone hardened. "Who was that?"

"He says he's one of the new rebel guys," Rama replied, his voice enthused. "I've heard many joined up last night after the word went out."

A sports car overtook Jen, with ease.

"Man, does he have solid wheels. Snazzy! Must be

loaded," Rama said as he followed.

Herby snorted. "Strange fellow, that."

❇ ❇ ❇ ❇ ❇ ❇

CHAPTER TWELVE

The Dragons

RAMA APPEARED LESS STRESSED as they drove behind Pierre. The storm eased off, and the rain dissipated. Kriaka smiled at the rainbow brightening up the late afternoon sky.

Thirty-minutes passed without incident; them following the red Mercedes, through the narrow muddy road worsened by the downpour. Not a soul was in sight.

Was that a flicker of lights? Or perhaps it's a mirage. Kriaka dismissed the distraction and continued to scan the scant surroundings.

Suddenly, a truck swerved out of hiding from the side of the road, and the sports car came to a screeching halt. Rama slammed on the brakes, stopping within a few centimeters from Pierre; she steadied herself and gasped.

"Ay. Oh no, it's the Dragons," Siya said.

Rama glanced at Kriaka.

"Shh," he whispered. Reaching for the secret side compartment below the steering wheel, he pulled out their father's handgun.

She shivered, and tapped his hand. "No, Rama."

He resisted for a moment, but clicked his tongue and yielded. She returned the weapon to the compartment and they sat tight.

The Dragon duo headed for their truck, long black jackets flowing around them, guns snug in their hip holsters. Behind them the leader's sleek leather coat blew in the wind. His weapon glistened as he approached Pierre. The two men engaged in conversation.

Kriaka's heart thumped. The duo reached Jen and the shorter Dragon veered to the left, his burning gaze fixed on her, until he passed and headed to the back window. She swallowed hard and dug her fingers into the seat. Behind her Shiana moaned and almost choked.

"Stay calm, Ana," she whispered.

The second Dragon, his jet-black hair falling sleekly over his ears, advanced toward Rama. She shook her head and urged him to stay calm, while the Dragon glowered over their bakkie.

"Hey, Saks!" he yelled. "Check out his side. There's someone in the backseat."

She froze as she glanced into the rearview mirror. The last time she checked with Herby, the blanket hid

Prince Jali, and Meosic and the food basket lay atop. She hoped nothing had changed since then. Her gaze met Herby's; he did not blink.

In the front, the sleek-haired Dragon fixed his stare on Rama, whose white-knuckled fingers gripped the steering wheel.

Saks pressed his hands on the back window, plastering his nose against it.

Meosic meowed and clawed at the glass, and the Dragon backed away and swore.

In the nick of time, the leader hollered from the Mercedes. "Come on, Dragons, there's nothing to be done here!"

Saks cursed again, spat, and kicked the tire. He signed a rude threat to Herby and Meosic, before punching Jen's roof, and storming off. The duo neared the sports car where Saks chatted to the leader. They turned and glared at the truck.

Pierre started his car and summoned Rama to follow him. Without hesitation, he revved Jen and raced behind, splattering mud around the Dragon trio. The leader stared at Herby, and Saks yelled obscenities at Meosic.

Shiana sniffled and Siya was blinking fast. "Hayibo."

At the back, Herby lifted the basket, and uncovered the prince. "He looks much better." Meosic purred from her spot at the prince's feet. "You clever cat. You saved us!" Herby said and rubbed her neck.

Rama let out a loud sigh. "I wonder what that Pierre told the leader? Isn't that Chan's son?"

"Ja—Michael. He does all his father's dirty work, though I heard he actually hates Chan," Herby replied. "I'm just glad they let us go!"

❄ ❄ ❄ ❄ ❄ ❄

CHAPTER THIRTEEN

Giant's Castle

J EN'S OCCUPANTS TRAVELED IN SILENCE, snuggled in the safety net cast by Pierre.

Kriaka pondered on their narrow escape. *I wonder how he learned about the First Ones?* She dismissed her nagging questions, grateful that he'd convinced Michael to let them through.

The rainbow's brilliant colors unraveled, flipping the sky to a passionate orange.

Siya as usual, grasped his chance to share anecdotes, his voice filled with enthusiasm. "History says, a long time ago, South Africa was called the rainbow nation."

"T-t-tell me s-s-something fun about the rainbow."

"Yebo, the ancient Greeks said the rainbow is a bridge between humanity and the best of the best world."

They passed through the real world instead and

Kriaka saddened. Little children, mostly stark naked, ran by the side of the road and yet they waved as Jen bumped through their impoverished villages.

Bony cows rested in the bare countryside. Young women trudged along the riverbank, balancing buckets of water on their heads, watched by elder men and women sitting on crooked porches of brown plaster houses.

The poverty throughout the villages overwhelmed her. *What have we let our world become?*

Ahead of Jen, Pierre competently swerved the fancy red Mercedes around the pothole-ridden road. One by one, the villages disappeared as Jen chugged behind the sports car toward the outline of the mountains.

Their mystical aura seemed to embrace her. Older and stronger than any of them, the ancient mountains continued to fascinate her. Their rugged peaks held a secret for sure.

A tiny creek wrapped around the foot of the rising rocks, and a blaring sign near the bank read "Private Fishery. Trespassers will be prosecuted."

Brisk fresh air, welcomed the weary troop entering the gravel road winding through the pass on the border of Basotho Land. They drove in awe of the fiery jagged tops of the Draco mountain, ablaze from the afternoon sun.

For an hour, they followed the creek winding their

way through the mountain, when Siya pushed his head between Kriaka and Rama and pointed.

"Look! There's the entrance to Giant's Castle!"

He continued in a high pitch, filled with excitement. "The cave is close by."

Jen labored, seemingly exhausted, and Rama patted her dashboard. "Hang in there, Jen."

They drove steadily down the tortuous road, close behind Pierre, to a boom gate beside a tiny tilted brick house. An elderly African gatekeeper hobbled out, and stretched his curved back, flashing a toothless grin at the two vehicles.

He lumbered over to Pierre, who chatted with him and pushed a stack of notes into his hand. The old man's eyes glazed. With effort, he opened the boom gates. Pierre drove through, leaned out his window, and watched them enter.

Siya saluted to the elderly man, and they received yet another grin.

Rama leaned out and waved to Pierre. "Thanks, bru, go ahead! Alert the others we're on our way. We gonna fill petrol here."

Pierre grinned and revved the Mercedes up the road.

"Yebo, good," the old man said. He shrugged. "Angaz, maybe no petrol tomorrow."

Rama reversed to a stained petrol stand propped

between two trees, at the side of the boom gates. "Wungani, fill it up, boss."

The old man nodded, his eyes upbeat. He opened the petrol cap, his wrinkled hands shaking as he started the machine.

"Wait a minute," Siya said.

Kriaka peered through the window, wondering what he was up to.

The boy forced his body against the rusty back door and jumped out. The old man grinned when he joined him and they spoke fast in Zulu. The elder rolled his eyes, shook his head strongly from side to side, and with his spare hand slapped Siya scoldingly on the head.

Rama kicked opened the driver door, but before he could get out, the boy signaled no, and all heads turned toward him and the old guard in heated discussion.

The man grabbed him close and whispered. The hushed conversation continued for several minutes, until a clanking alerted the guard. He removed the petrol filler, tightened Jen's cap, and patted Siya on the shoulder.

The boy bowed. "Siya bonga."

Rama paid for the petrol, and the man waved goodbye as they continued up the road in the nature reserve.

"Well Siya?" Rama prompted in an eager tone.

The boy cleared his throat and whispered, "The road

to the cave washed away last week in the mountain storm."

Kriaka caught her breath.

"W-what if Prince J-J-Jali dies?" Shiana choked back a sob.

Siya intervened. "Hayibo, no, the elder, he told me how to get to the cave, and it's shorter!"

Rama laughed. "Heck, child, you scared the skin out of me. Okay, lead the way."

Sighs of relief echoed through the truck, and Siya poked his head between Kriaka and Rama, pointing the way down a red sand path, leading in to a side road through the mountain forest.

"Man, this is donga land for sure!" Rama drove Jen like a dodgem car, avoiding most of the crater-like potholes deepened by the storm.

Kriaka breathed easier. "Thank goodness the storm stopped." She glanced at the back. "We've enough time to settle in Prince Jali before meeting the Firs—" She lunged forward and reached out in time before they screeched to a halt.

Siya flew through the gap between Rama and her, and steadied himself.

"Oh, man!" Rama said.

Ahead of them, a large herd of baboons blocked the forest path.

"Keep the windows closed!" Rama shouted.

Kriaka turned to assure Shiana of their safety, but her sister appeared unperturbed.

Herby as usual rounded his lips to blow her a kiss, when a sound at his side distracted him. He pulled off the blanket covering the prince.

"Tuttles." The prince's soft voice filled the air.

As if at his beckoning, the largest baboon sauntered to the side where he lay, and struck the window, rocking the whole truck. It peered at the little prince. The baboons joined him, each taking turns to look in at the prince.

The lead baboon let out a penetrating scream and beat at his chest, moving his arms up and down, with the gang of baboons following suit.

"They are bowing!" Siya said. "Hayibo, wow!"

"They like Prince J-J-Jali." A radiant smile lit up Shiana's face.

"Tuttles, Tuttles!" the prince repeated.

Rama raised his hands in disbelief. "Well, I ain't waitin' to find out if they like him or not." He steered through the unobstructed path ahead, leaving the baboons behind.

Kriaka patted his shoulder and pointed to the pine trees on each side of the path. Their branches swayed in rhythm and cones rained onto Jen. But Rama remained tight-lipped.

They continued to edge their way through the rugged path deeper into the forest, until Siya pointed ahead, and they came to a halt.

"Yebo, yes," Siya said. "This is it." He kicked open his door and sprang out to inspect the surroundings.

Shiana, Rama, and Kriaka joined him. He directed them to a sloped trail to the left. "There, see, we walk up there."

They followed his pointing, to the top.

"There's the opening to the cave!" He said, and without waiting for their approval, disappeared into the trail.

"Let's settle the boys up there, then," Rama said, and opened the back of the truck.

Herby smiled at them, and nodded toward the prince, still stretched out on the seat. His skin color had returned to normal. And as if aware of their fascination with him, his head moved, and his eyelids fluttered.

He looked at Kriaka. "Mama, it is you," he said, before he closed his eyes and drifted off.

✳ ✳ ✳ ✳ ✳ ✳

CHAPTER FOURTEEN

Cat Alliance

MAMA!

The prince's utterance rang in Kriaka's head as Rama lifted the boy and carried him up the trail. Herby's eyes glistened. He hugged her and planted a tender kiss on her forehead, before they removed supplies for the night, and hastened to the calls of Siya already at the top of the trail.

He shouted from the branch of a tree and waved down to them still at the foot of the trail. "Found it!"

Shiana, motivated by Meosic speeding ahead, huffed and puffed behind Kriaka. Rama, the first one to join Siya at the top, carefully surveyed the plateau.

Siya jumped from the tree and led the way into a high cave. "It's still dry!" He brushed a layer of leaves from a flat rock inside the deep, cold grotto.

The coolness should help the prince's temperature, Kriaka thought as she unpacked a few cotton blankets from the crinkled duffel bag hanging on Herby's shoulder. Unable to resist the temptation, she held the knitted quilt to her face, and a wave of nostalgia swept over her. She missed her parents dreadfully. They had rescued so many abandoned children in their short lives, and today it seemed as if they were right here with her to comfort the lost prince.

She hummed their song of freedom, while she prepared a bed of blankets on the rock for their unexpected visitor, Prince Jali.

Meosic snuggled at the boy's feet, and apparently comforted by her presence, the prince smiled in his sleep.

Did that dot on his forehead move a little, yet again? She dismissed the thought and unpacked the food and water.

Herby assessed the prince. "It's remarkable. His temperature is normalizing!"

Rama's agitated voice hurried them. "Come on, we gotta get to the meeting, before we're missed." He helped Kriaka unpack the emergency lanterns.

"Siya, you've gotta turn on the lights only when it gets really dark. Can you take care of the boy and the whole setup here?"

"Yebo, Rama, don't worry, we'll be fine. Do you know—?"

"Do you know that we have no contact with you until we get back?" He stared at Siya.

"Yebo."

Kriaka touched the prince's head. *Be safe, little one.*

"Come, M-Meosic," Shiana called to her sand cat, but she did not budge.

They had no option but to accept her affinity for the lost prince, as she curled up below his bed and watched them wave goodbye.

Herby went ahead, and every now and then reached back to guide Shiana down the steep trail. Around them the forest began to settle into its evening rhythms. Kriaka sighed deeply, she always felt at peace in this environment.

Rama had already readied Jen when they approached the base of the trail. His fingers rapped on the steering wheel and they rushed into the truck.

Kriaka leaned out the window and waved to Siya at the top of the trail. She hoped that the boys would be okay on their own. *Wait a minute, something seemed different up there.* A cluster of trees fenced the area around the cave, and a flock of multicolored feathered friends settled on the treetop where Siya was perched.

She twisted her lip in disbelief and turned to Rama. But the narrow path en route to the main hut and their apocalyptic world seemed to weigh heavily on him.

With the unexpected princely distraction, they had lost track of the real reason for their trip to Giant's Castle. She sighed. They were finally on their way to the momentous meeting.

✻ ✻ ✻ ✻ ✻ ✻

CHAPTER FIFTEEN

The Missing Prince

SIYA WAITED UNTIL THE LAST CHUG of Jen's engine melted into the forest. He swung down the tree and landed with a thud.

Those group of trees weren't there before! Hayibo!

A troop of squirrels gathered where the entrance of the cave once was. Even in the last speck of sunset, red, orange, and yellow butterflies were clearly visible on the flowered ferns hanging over where the cave had opened. So many trees, so many bushes, so many creatures.

What's going on? *Where's the opening?* He poked around, until the thick carpet of ferns gave way to the cave.

He stood in amazement, made a full turn to scan the outside, before lifting the plush cover off the entrance.

The ferns flapped firmly on his back, pushing him into the cave. Remarkably, the door did not darken the cave! Instead, a glimmer of soft lights welcomed him. But he had not turned on the lamps. The glow was coming from the ceiling, where a host of fireflies flitted.

His heart raced, and he rushed to the rock bed. Empty. *I lost the prince!*

He slapped his face hard. *Idiot, domkop!* He searched, panic-stricken. There, on one side of the cave, stood the prince, surrounded by birds and squirrels. Fireflies danced above his head, and Meosic purred by his feet. The prince's gaze fixed on him. Siya drew in a quick breath and ran toward the silent figure.

"Hayibo, I didn't lose you! Wow, Prince," he said, and again slapped his face as he danced around the figure. "How you feeling?"

No response.

Oh no, he's become a zombie!

"Your body, it's hurting? Are you okay?" He stopped his ramblings. A nervous smile edged upward on his stinging face, and he stared at the still form. *Hayibo, I hope it's not a ghost!* He slapped his face even harder.

❉ ❉ ❉ ❉ ❉ ❉

CHAPTER SIXTEEN

Princess Reena

JALI WATCHED AS SIYA ran around him. *What an odd boy.* His dark brown hands moved back and forth, slapping his face every so often.

Ooka, he does not have a Third Eye.

Perhaps he needed to console the boy and stop him from hurting his face.

"Siya, I am well. Thank you for taking such good care of me. My temperature is regulated."

The boy grinned, flashed his shiny white teeth, and danced. He smacked his head and rushed to the items near the rock from where Jali had risen, and brought him an object.

"Water, amanzi," Siya said, encouraging him to accept it. "Doc said you must drink lots of water. Take it, take the bottle."

Jali tilted his head and hesitated before accepting it.

He pressed the bottle, it squeaked and crinkled. Befuddled, he watched Siya. The boy turned the narrow end of his bottle. It popped. He removed the top, slanted the bottle toward his mouth, and drank.

Siya stopped. "Hayibo, sorry, sorry." The boy hooked his empty bottle between his legs, repeated the process with Jali's bottle, and handed it to him.

He imitated, emptying the bottle and licking his lips.

"Water bottle," he said.

Siya laughed. "Yebo, water bottle, water bottle." He dashed off and returned with another bottle. This time Jali opened it and guzzled.

He pointed to the empty cave. "Where are the other two-eyed people, Kriaka Adi, Rama Adi, Shiana, and Doctor Herby?"

Siya chuckled, bopped his head crazily, and calmed. "Off to important meeting with the First Ones."

Jali looked around the cave. He missed Zooka. "I must talk to Reena. The Zookian Glass—"

Meosic meowed and the birds fluttered. A dazzling blue light filled the cave, and Siya dropped the empty bottle.

"Reena!" Jali ran to the Zookian Glass. Reena and Commander ZW1 were in the Control Chamber. They wore worried expressions on their faces.

"Jali, you are stabilized. Your thermo has regulated."

"Reena, what is happening?"

"Prince Jali, you are safe for now," Commander ZW1 replied.

"Are you okay, Reena? What happened? Why am I here?"

"An unidentified radiation interfered with the Transporter. We were prevented from entering the planet and the Transporter triggered a destruction sequence, trapping us. You courageously reached in and tried to save the Magnificent ZW7 and me. But you switched places. Jali, you beamed over, and we were left behind."

His heart pounded and his ears twitched. "When can you beam here, Reena? When can I return to Zooble?"

She frowned and Commander ZW1 interjected. "Prince Jali, all efforts at reconstructing the Transporter have failed. Magnificent ZW7 are working continuously to mold a robust super-vision to overcome the complications of planet Earth's radiation field. Our immediate concern is to beam you back to Zooble. Princess Reena and our team will continue our mission after we regenerate our Transporter."

"Jali, we are ready to extract you right away," Reena said.

Relieved, he smiled and turned to Siya, still frozen at the corner of the cave.

"Siya, I must depart now. I thank you and Kriaka

Adi, Rama Adi, Shiana, Doctor Herby, and Meosic for your hospitality and assistance." He held the bottle close. "May I take the water bottle with me?"

The boy sagged his shoulders. He dragged his feet and looked at the Zookian Glass and back at Jali. "You are leaving us." His mouth turned down.

"Yes, Siya, I must. Do not be concerned. My sister, the great Protector, Princess Reena, and the Magnificent ZW7 warriors will beam over as soon as they can. Their mission is to rescue your beings."

Jali bolted to the center of the cave. The fireflies fluttered around and the birds and squirrels gathered close. Meosic curled her tail around Siya.

"Prepare to transport, Prince Jali," Reena commanded. The Zookian Glass faded.

A bright white light surrounded Jali. He smiled, tapped his feet, and waved to Siya, who hesitated before waving back.

Ring One descended on Jali. It swirled round and round and round...

Ring Two descended.

Ring Three descended.

The Three Rings swirled.

Faster.

And faster.

Again, round and round and round the Three Rings

swirled.

A red light sparked, crackled, and burst.

Darkness filled the cave.

✳ ✳ ✳ ✳ ✳ ✳

CHAPTER SEVENTEEN

My Space Friend

SIYA CROUCHED, COVERED HIS eyes from the blinding light, and turned away.

The birds fluttered and chirped in frenzy, and the squirrels hid behind the bed, as Meosic clung to his ankle.

Sheer darkness replaced the cheerful lights, and a hollow throb clawed at his stomach. His space friend was gone. Tears rolled down his face, and onto the water bottle. His firm grip crushed the container; Meosic meowed and jumped up.

He grasped the distorted form, and shut his eyes in an effort to block out the sorrow. He wiped his wet face. The birds scattered past his cheek, and a cool breeze swept over his body. Reluctantly, he dragged open his heavy eyelids and adjusted to the dark cave.

Light crept in. Fireflies spotlighted the center of the

cave where the rings had disappeared.

He squinted, and jumping up he sprinted to the spot. Curled in a bundle on the floor lay the prince!

✽ ✽ ✽ ✽ ✽ ✽

CHAPTER EIGHTEEN

The Portal

A HAND GRIPPED JALI'S SHOULDER, and he opened his eyes. "Reena." He tried to see through the dim light as he touched the hand.

"Prince," whispered a soft voice. "Are you okay?"

Siya! Oh no, I did not beam over.

A shiver ran down his spine, and he closed his eyes. Painful sobs racked his body. He tried to clear his head.

"This is a dream. This is a dream. Reena, Grandma, wake me up. I must have eaten too much cacao cake. Wake me up. Do not leave me behind!"

Hands shook him gently. "Prince, please wake up. Are you okay? Please be okay." Siya's teardrop splattered on his face and his cries wrenched at him.

The lost prince looked up into the depth of Siya's big, black, tear-filled eyes and calmness blanketed the two little boys, cradling them with infinite love. They reached for each other and clung tightly.

Birds chirped and fluttered around the figures on the floor of the cave in the heart of Africa. Squirrels skipped at their feet, starry fireflies danced above their heads, and Meosic stretched her neck and meowed a song of hope. The cave filled with fauna and flora; they shadow-danced on the ceiling. The Cosmos had come to them.

The boys held hands in the middle of the grotto, looked around at the wild party, and burst into laughter. The ferns had crept in and painted the walls grass green. Their white flowers peered from the entrance. The pair laughed again.

Siya turned to Jali, took a deep bow, looked up, and winked.

"Prince Jali, welcome to South Africa, where we jol in style!"

The boy swiveled in the air, and danced around him, bending his legs low, swinging his arms and kicking high. Jali joined in and they roared with laughter.

In a few minutes, the party quieted and the squirrels and birds gathered around the boys. Jali stood motionless—so many eyes fixed on him.

"Prince, I think your sister Princess Reena has problems with getting you back, ja."

"Yes, Siya, you are correct."

Siya spoke with determination. "Tell me how I can

help."

Jali looked around; every gaze was set on him.

"How can we help you, Prince?" echoed the birds, squirrels, and fireflies.

"First step," he said, "I *must* counsel with Reena immediately."

Feeling confident, he stood in the middle of the cave, closed his two eyes, and took a deep breath. Rejuvenated by the energy all around him, he focused his own energy on his Third Eye.

And he waited.

An intense blue light filled the grotto. Siya gasped, and the creatures squealed with delight as the Zookian Glass emerged.

Reena materialized with Commander ZW1, who paced back and forth. "Prince Jali, the Zookian Transporter is dysfunctional," he said. "We cannot extract you from the planet, nor can we transport Princess Reena to you."

Jali felt an emptiness deep within him.

"Brother, listen, for now we encounter the problem with the Transporter."

His shoulders drooped and the hollowness inside him worsened.

"We counseled with Grandma and Protector 1," Reena said.

"Grandma?" His heart raced.

She smiled and spoke with excitement. "We are advised that there is a location, a short distance from you, that holds a Portal. But you need the assistance of the purest of Earth beings to unlock the Gateway to it, and create the perfect transportation conditions."

He stood on tiptoes; his Third Eye fluttered. "Yes, Reena, I can do it."

His new followers cheered around him. He took on a regal stance and pushed his chest out. "Reena, what are the coordinates for the location?"

She smiled and winked.

"28°46'21.07"S-28°52'21.72"E in the Mont Aux Sources, where the three rivers for the country of South Africa once rose. Within is a cave; the energy is astronomical and prime for transportation in seven Earth days, Prince Jali," Commander ZW1 said.

"Jee, time is short. The sooner we extract you, the sooner we beam to planet Earth, the sooner we can rescue the beings. Use your Zookian capabilities, my dear brother."

His Third Eye fluttered; a rush of energy rose within him. "I will rally the beings, find the Mont Aux Sources and prepare the Portal for the exchange, Princess Reena," he replied, in the manner of a gallant Zookian warrior.

She smiled, and saluted. "Zookian wishes to you,

Prince Jali, and to your team."

Siya bowed. The creatures drew closer, and they cheered as the transmission ended.

Jali turned, to find all gazes glued on him, and his little heart drummed. He straightened his shoulders and spoke in a regal tone. "Fellow Earth beings, we have a vital mission to accomplish to save your planet. Are you with me?"

"Yes, Prince Jali!" the beings roared.

"Yes, Prince Jali!" Siya said.

"Our founding purest Earth team comprises those gathered here today. You spread the word, we need help from ever pure creature on your planet. I shall counsel with Siya."

The beings curtsied and exited, leaving behind a troop of fireflies to create light. Meosic stood guard at the cave entrance.

Siya blinked nonstop. "Hayibo Prince, you talk to the animals and trees and birds?"

Jali wrinkled his eyebrows, puzzled. "You cannot?"

The boy turned his palms up. "Aikona, no, nobody here talks to the animals or birds. Well, Shiana whispers to them all the time, but I don't hear them talking back. I chat sometimes when I am lonely, but they ignore me."

"Can you not hear them talk to me?"

"No, aikona!"

The fern door to the cave gave way and Jali walked out, Siya ran behind him.

"Teach me, Prince, to talk to the animals and to know what they say to me."

"That is beyond me. On Zooka, everyone can talk to each other."

Siya placed his hands on either side of his head and rocked side to side. "Hayibo." He lowered his hands, and nodded with a serious look on his face. "Yebo, abaningi amandla."

"Yes, many powers," Jali replied.

"Hayibo, you can understand Zulu too!"

"Is that the name of your language? Can you not align your speech?"

"Naaaa, aikona. Prince, tell me about where you come from?"

"You must be specific. What do you want to know?"

The boy scratched his head and paced. He glanced up, paced around once more, and lowering his gaze he whispered. "Do you have superpowers?"

"Define superpowers."

"Yebo, like a superhero, you know, can you fly?"

Jali lowered his gaze and sighed. "Not yet. My sister Reena, my Grandma, and other Zookians can."

Siya frowned. "When will you fly?"

Jali twirled his fingers, stared out at the Cosmos, and

heaved a deep sigh. "When I graduate from Level-4. I tried two times already. That I kept failing concerned me, therefore I created a special bond with Tuttles, to help me fly." He puckered his lips, and his eyes lit up. "When I get back on Zooble, I shall complete the practice sessions with Guardian 1, and when Reena returns from your planet, I will graduate!"

"Yebo, I wish they taught us to fly at the schools here. And Prince, what's Tuttles?"

At the mention of Tuttles, Jali's heart lightened. "He is my best friend; wise. And yes, he can fly."

"And Prince, what about Zooble?"

The boy followed Jali's gaze to the distant sky. "She is our intergalactic space explorer, a bubble created and propelled by visionary powers. Reena, Commander ZW1 and the Magnificent ZW7 warriors travel in her to reach other planets and galaxies for rescue missions."

"Ay, so that's how you came here—with your sister in the bubble Zooble?"

Jali turned to the boy, who had a twinkle in his eyes. "Siya, where do you live? Where is your family?"

The boy's face saddened. He stooped and gathered a handful of twigs and grass. He remained silent, staring at the stars, before shrugging.

He lifted himself onto a large boulder at the cave entrance. Jali joined him, and the fireflies hovered above the silent pair.

"I have no family, now," Siya said. "I've been living in caves for a long time."

✳ ✳ ✳ ✳ ✳ ✳

CHAPTER NINETEEN

Ghosts from the Past

SIYA CHOKED BACK A CRY, trying to be strong in front of his new superhero friend.

The prince looked at him. "You have no family, no sister, no brother, no grandma?"

"Nobody."

The boys dangled their feet from the rock and stared at the forest below them. Above their heads, the fireflies flickered, and around the cave little squirrels scurried, stopped, winked at the prince and sped on.

Siya let out a deep sigh, grateful for the prince, his amazing buddy from the skies. A petal drifted onto his lap. He smelled it and shared the sweet aroma from the red rose petal with the prince, who smiled with delight and closed his eyes.

The young African boy was ready to share his pain

with his superhero. "I used to live in Umlazi township with my mommy, daddy, my big brother Vincent, and my uncle—my father's brother." His gaze wandered to the treetops as he remembered the forest around the shack where they lived. "My daddy was a taxi driver, and my mommy cleaned the houses of the rich ones, you know, the laanis."

He swallowed hard. "One day, my mommy didn't come home. Daddy went all the way to the laanis' house to find her. The boss's guards, they threw him out. Said that she won't be coming home no more." He sniffed and clenched his teeth to stop the sobs.

"Late that night, Daddy went back to the big boss's house, and he saw Mommy, but it was too late. Before he could drag her out, the guards, they beat him up and threw him in the ditch by the railway lines. My uncle, he found him and brought him home. He was hurt bad, but nobody in our township had money for the doctor. I watched him through the door with the sangoma. He called me and Vincent. Said we must stay away from the big boss, said they were doing bad things with our people. He told us to run away and hide."

He wiped the flood of tears off his face and sniveled. "After a day, he died. Vincent and me, we walked all night. We jumped on trucks and hid in the trains. We heard my uncle disappeared. I was frightened and tired, and I held Vincent's hand so tight. In Chatsworth, we lived with the Unit 1 street beggars. Vincent said I must hang around the schools and build my brain—maybe then we can escape. Every day he found food, and we slept in drain holes and caves.

"One day, no Vincent." Sobs overpowered him. "I didn't know what to do. I didn't know where to go. I started walking, and walking, and stopped in Arena Park." He wiped his face again. "I stuck around the schools, hid in the labs. I wanted to learn so when Vincent came back he would be proud of my brain. One day, Shiana, she saw me digging for food in the school bin. She saved me. Shiana saved me!" His sobs racked his entire body, and he bent over.

And wept.

Small hands rested on his shoulders and tenderly pulled him close. He leaned his head on the chest of his space prince, and they both sobbed.

✳ ✳ ✳ ✳ ✳ ✳

While he opened his heart to the prince, Siya had woven a holder of twigs and grass.

"Prince, I think you like this cup."

He sprang up and returned with the food bag that Kriaka had packed. He emptied the water bottle into the prince's new cup and handed the prince the best yellow mango from the pack of fruits. His friend analyzed the skin, sniffed, and nibbled. His green eyes beamed.

In the middle range of the Draco mountains, outside their stone cave lit with fireflies and surrounded by forest beings, the two boys ate their first meal together under the glittering stars in Giant's Castle.

✳ ✳ ✳ ✳ ✳ ✳

CHAPTER TWENTY

Alien Language

"WHAT ABOUT YOUR MOMMY AND DADDY, Prince? Are they on Zooka?" Siya asked.

Jali's breathing slowed, and he shrugged. "The details remain unclear. I have been counseled by our Royal Guardian that two weeks following my birth, my parents were called on a rescue mission and did not return."

The young prince tried to sound brave. "My Grandma, Queen Vraka, reared my sister and me. That is all I know." His ears perked and his super-hearing activated. "Siya, something approaches."

The boy clawed his way up the closest tree, alighted on a thick branch, and strained his neck. He looked down at him and disagreed, but waited and watched through the forest.

Within a few minutes, creaks and voices flowed up to them. Meosic ran to the edge of the plateau.

Shiana's head popped up. "Hello, M-Meosic," she said with an energized voice. Her gaze met Jali's and she curtsied, before looking up at the fireflies hovering throughout the plateau.

Rama Adi emerged next. "Kid, you okay?" He ripped off his cap and wiped his forehead. He ruffled Jali's hair, and dug into the bag of food.

Kriaka Adi smiled when she ascended. "Prince Jali." She bowed.

Meosic, already pampered by Shiana, purred with delight. "Meo, you like P-Prince Jali, I see. Go f-find your dinner, then come back for some water." The sand cat ran off behind the cave.

Doctor Herby, the last one off the trail, holding rolls of papyrus, grinned at the sight of Jali.

"Prince Jali, how has Siya been treating you?" He touched his forehead. "Your temperature is stable now." And he patted his cheek.

Rama threw the doctor a food pack, and turned to the entrance of the cave. "Hey, what's going on here?" He lifted the fern door. The group followed him into the cave, glowing like a sunny summer morning.

"I told you the prince is special. He talks to animals. They love him!" Siya responded in a high-pitched voice.

Rama frowned and squinted, letting out a grunt, while Herby stared around the cave, with a look of amazement.

"But of course Prince Jali does," Kriaka said, cheering Jali.

Siya filled them in on the Zookian Glass and failed attempt to beam him.

"So, Princess says we must gather at the Mont Aux Sources—28°46′21.07″S   28°52′21.72″E—in seven days, with pure beings. The Portal will open and Prince Jali can beam to their spaceship Zooble, and Princess Reena and the Magnificent team can help rescue us and our planet!"

Rama devoured his sandwich. "Heh, don't tell me you saw them in the hologram again!"

"Yebo, and they can fly on their planet!"

"Okay, I get it," Rama said. He grabbed Siya and tickled his sides.

"Hayibo!" The boy giggled.

"Well, Siya, did you pinch yourself when all this was happening?" Rama asked.

Siya clicked his tongue. "Hayibo. How do you think the fireflies came, heh?" He rolled his eyes and rocked his head left and right.

Jali smiled, and his loyal set of fireflies twinkled above his head and throughout the cave.

Rama moaned, and pursed his lips behind Kriaka,

who was watching Jali intently.

"Prince Jali, is what Siya saying right?" she asked.

"Yes, Kriaka Adi." He drew closer to her, and the fireflies followed his gait.

"We have to take you to Mont Aux Sources and gather with pure beings so that the Portal opens for you to exchange places with Princess Reena?"

He confirmed her summary. Squirrels rallied at his feet, and Meosic purred. One squirrel ran up his arm and leaped onto the cat's back. *She must be Brela's cousin.*

Siya danced up and down and stayed close to him.

The rest of the group stared at them.

"Kriaka Adi, Siya's report is correct. Queen Vraka, my grandmother, received an SOS from someone on your planet. My sister, Princess Reena, and the Zookian warriors were dispatched to rescue your planet. Through an accident in the Transporter, I beamed over instead of them."

"You were not supposed to be here, Prince Jali?" Kriaka asked, with a look of shock.

He confirmed her deduction.

"SOS from whom?" She turned and looked at each of the troop. "Who sent the SOS?"

They shrugged.

A shiver ran down Jali's spine. "Kriaka Adi, your team did not transmit the SOS?"

"No, Prince Jali, we did not." She frowned. "Princess Reena and the Zookian warriors have been sent to rescue our planet?"

"Yes, Kriaka Adi, the Peace-Keeping Force spreads bliss in the Cosmos,"

"Prince Jali," she whispered. "This Zooble, is it now close to us?"

"Yes, Kriaka Adi, due to damage to the Transporter, they can beam to your planet precisely at the ordained spot on the specific time after extracting me."

A stunned silence filled the cave.

Herby rushed to her side. "But this is great! They can find the GIFT!"

Rama placed his hands on his hips. "They can zap the whole of the Dragons gang, and kill that Chan and his evil following once and for all."

Siya whispered. "Hayibo. They can find my brother."

But Rama sneered and the excitement quickly changed. He locked his arms behind his back. "Wait a minute, now. For one thing, this hologram stuff happens when we're not looking, and only the kids have seen it, right?"

"S-Siya says th-th-they speak another language!" Shiana said.

Rama's eyes widened. "Heh, gotcha now." He approached Jali. "I say, kiddo, is this true? You can speak another language?"

Jali frowned. "All languages."

Rama spun around and chuckled. "Well, let's hear it then, and we'll know for sure, yeah. Let's hear you speak your alien lingo!"

Okay, they want me to talk in Zookish — sure, why not?

Shiana and Siya edged closer, prompting him to disprove Rama's skepticism once and for all.

"On planet Zooka, this is the language we speak. It is called Zookish!" He spoke, with assurance.

A short silence followed, before Rama's laughter echoed through the cave. Shiana and Siya pouted, and his ears tingled.

Herby looked down and remained silent. Kriaka rushed to Jali and hugged him.

But Rama continued to laugh and snigger. "Well, here on planet Earth, kid, we call that English!" He kicked a pebble and turned his nose up at him.

Siya agreed. "Yebo, Prince, only English coming out!"

Oh no! He squeezed his eyes tight. *It made sense.* Why did he not think of it before? He remembered Reena's report from her first intergalactic mission. Zookish was the secret language of Zookian natives; concealed from non-Zookians for reasons still unknown to him.

Comfortable with the truth, he nestled in Kriaka's

loving embrace.

"It's okay, Prince. You're under great stress. Who wouldn't be if they were stranded and trapped on an alien, unfriendly planet like ours?"

Rama's laughter stopped, he plonked onto the bed and stared at Jali.

Fireflies haloed his head, and his troop of squirrels and birds rallied at his feet. The lead squirrel stood tall on Meosic.

Everyone looked at Rama and waited.

He rose, extending his muscular arms and adjusting his cap. He shot a glance at Jali.

"All right, let's focus," he said to Herby and Kriaka. "Tonight, we instructed the First Ones to scout underground for the GIFT's location. These two hundred troopers are loyal and determined. I've no intention of calling them off, let alone telling them about a make-believe Zoob hanging out in space waiting to rescue us. They'll think I've gone cuckoo!"

He waited for a response then continued.

"I ain't gonna call them off, and I'm not sure about this great rescue mission by the Zooks! I've not seen any hologram and definitely no superpowers. Heck, there's not even Zookish. Yeah, and who sent the SOS?"

He twirled his hand, and crinkled his forehead in response to their silence.

"If it was one of our troops, we'd know. Something's fishy! I say we continue with our plan, and find out where the GIFT is. The GIFT is all we have."

He sat on the boulder and stared at them.

Jali's heart sank into a bottomless pit.

Kriaka wandered over to Rama. "I agree—we don't stop the troop's plan. Brother, we all want to find the GIFT for the sake of our future." She knelt and held his hands. "I know if Mom and Dad were here, they too would want us to hunt for the GIFT." She turned to Jali. "But, they would also want us to help a lost child to find his way home." She laid her hand on Rama's chest. "We can do both."

Rama listened without interrupting.

"Brother, I know deep down you feel the way I do about the young one who's been trusted in our care. I've lived my life rescuing those who need help." She looked at Shiana. "I think we must help Prince Jali return to his family."

Kriaka rose and looked at each of them. She clasped her palms together and closed her eyes.

"And besides, I know the location of the Mont Aux Sources Portal to which Prince Jali refers."

✳ ✳ ✳ ✳ ✳ ✳

CHAPTER TWENTY-ONE

The GIFT Of Life

JALI CAUGHT HIS BREATH.

Herby edged closer to Kriaka and touched her shoulders. "You do?"

She nodded. "The Portal is within the strongest vibrating spot in South Africa. How would the Zookians know about it? Nobody has figured it out." She looked at Rama. "And I haven't revealed it to anyone, not even to the ones I love."

She placed a hand on his chest, and with the other she touched the doctor's face.

The men appeared mesmerized by her words.

"I've had a good feeling about Prince Jali from the second I saw him hunched over Siya."

Jali felt a calmness descend over him. *Yes, there was hope.*

She turned to him and smiled. "Us finding the GIFT is somehow linked to us helping him. He is a lost child, wanting to go home. We must reunite him with his family. Agreed?"

Herby consented without hesitation.

Everyone looked to Rama.

"Agreed," he whispered.

Jali smiled with happiness. *I can go home.*

Kriaka reached into Herby's bag, taking out a lightly colored cloth. "Why don't you men figure out the plan? I want to speak to Prince Jali."

She parted the fern gate, and Jali walked out with her into the hum of the forest. Outside the cave, Meosic curled her tail around his leg, and he stopped. The lead squirrel had perched herself atop the cat.

"Hello, are you Brela's cousin?" He asked. "I'll call you Brelize." She stood on her hind legs and bowed.

Kriaka smiled, "I see you are feeling more comfortable on our planet, Prince Jali." She handed him the item she had taken from the bag. "Just in case, this jacket and hood will hide your ears and dot." She draped the jacket over him. "Fits well. See this hood?" She pulled it over his head. "There, now you look like any other Earth boy."

His heart bloomed with delight. *I look like an Earth boy!*

She touched his cheek. "Prince Jali, how are you feeling?"

"I am fully recovered, Kriaka Adi." But his mind was fixated on what had transpired in the cave. He needed clarity on the point of extraction. "Would you clarify your secret insights about the Portal at Mont Aux Sources. Have you visited there previously?"

She smiled. "Prince Jali, from the time I was little, I've dreamed of strange numbers—28 46 21 07 52 21 72. They made no sense until I became a teacher of science and learned to read maps, the longitudes and latitudes. No, I've not yet been to the spot, but I can picture it clearly. It's in a hidden area of the ancient mountain. I've never dared draw it, or write it down, or even know why I feared doing so. I didn't understand it till now."

The chirp of the birds, and trills of the crickets merged with the night sounds, as they walked the stony path near the cave.

"Kriaka Adi, do you miss your parents?"

"Yes, every second of every day."

"What happened to them?"

She sighed and linked arms with him.

"They were leaders of the First Ones." Her hold on him tightened, and she lowered her head on his. "Chan's Dragons executed them ten years ago in front of Rama."

He cringed, and her arms quickly comforted him.

"Rama vowed revenge on Chan and his Dragons, the evil force that has been gathering power not just here, but also around the planet. They make guinea pigs of anyone who opposes them. They've been known to use them to test secret technologies for interplanetary occupation." Her voice brightened. "Herby keeps Rama centered. Yes, my Herb, he's always calm and clear-headed. We plan to marry after we find the GIFT."

"What is the GIFT, Kriaka Adi?"

She made way for him on the big boulder. Meosic curled at her feet, and Brelize ran up his arm and settled in his Earth-boy hood.

"The GIFT is our precious stone that will carry the pure ones to a place of happiness, where everyone laughs, has no hatred—"

"Like Zooka?"

She tilted her head. "Is that the magical utopian place where you are from, Prince Jali?"

He nodded.

"Where did you find the GIFT, Kriaka Adi?"

"Hmmm, ever since I could remember, my mother carried a little white stone with her. When she and I meditated together each day, she would bless me with the stone, saying it was our key to bliss. I could've sworn that each year on my birthday the GIFT glowed. Then my parents sent Rama away to study in the US, which I suspect was done to keep his hot temper in check. A few years later, Herb sent Rama a message that he was needed back home. I was sent to the US, and the tragedy happened ten years after that, just as Rama began leading the First Ones. When I came home, I found the stone. Mother had buried it in our secret place in the rose garden. Each time I meditated, I felt its powers expand, and my dreams of the future became clearer. Before I knew it, the GIFT was being sought by the Dragons. One day it disappeared."

"Kriaka Adi, who stole the GIFT?"

She shrugged. "All I know is, I wished with all my might that we find our precious stone. Then you appeared."

He sighed. He missed Grandma and Reena.

"You have to get back home, Prince Jali."

"Yes I have to."

"Don't you worry—we'll return you to your family again."

They sat in silence, basking in the glory of the serene night, ablaze with fireflies.

His ears perked and his super-hearing triggered. He pointed over her shoulder. "Someone is coming."

"Here? That's impossible. No one knows about this place." She gathered Meosic and looked around. "Quick, get inside!"

His Third Eye fluttered as she tugged him into the cave.

"We've been discovered! Hide the prince!"

"Hide!"

＊ ＊ ＊ ＊ ＊ ＊

End of Book i: Dance of Fireflies

Taming The Impostor Saga
Adventure Time Travel Fantasy Series

Read On

✻ ✻ ✻ ✻ ✻ ✻

SPECIAL GIFTS FOR YOU

I hope you enjoyed ᴅance of fɪᴇflieꜱ Book i in Taming The Impostor Saga Fantasy Adventure.

I'd love for you to **Leave Your Review**.

Would you like to **join my VIP Team of First Readers** for upcoming books?

DrVie.com/ARC-Team

Would you like to know more about the series?

DrVie.com/Taming-The-Impostor-map

GIFTS FOR YOU

Receive your **free short story:**

Prequel to Taming The Impostor Saga

and special deals on my books.

DrVie.com/VIPfreebooks

❊ ❊ ❊ ❊ ❊ ❊

CONNECT WITH ME

I'd love to be of help to you and loved ones.
DrVie.com (main site)
facebook.com/ScientistDoctorVie
twitter.com/DrVie
Youtube.com/DrVieSuperfoods
Enjoy more EBooks, AudioBooks and Paperbacks:
Taming The Impostor Saga
Alkona Book ii
Wunamangaz Book iii
The Pure Ones Books i-iii
Thank you for your support, which helps me mentor
thousands of youth for free through my global Super-
Conscious Humanity Youth Program

✳ ✳ ✳ ✳ ✳ ✳

ABOUT DR. SHERI VIE

My dear Reader,

Life sure is an adventure, even with family and friends.

For me, my youthful adventures really began solo when I left South Africa to study in the USA-certainly uncommon in those days, for a single Indian female.

Since then, I've been living in six countries, twenty plus cities...on my own. A real-life adventure; new places, a variety of people, numerous cultures, exotic foods, foreign languages and of course endless challenges.

What truly amazed me beyond the fascinating cities, towns and traditions, were the breathtaking natural environments as I hiked high up in the mountain trails around the globe, sometimes with a guide and most often on my own. The African ranges to the Himalayan peaks. Pristine air, sounds of nature, and the splendor of fauna and flora in their natural habitat resonated with me. Staring into the eyes of a young deer, strolling alongside a giraffe, and reveling in the dainty clasp of a humming bird on my finger.

When I'm not exploring mountains, I share stories of my adventures to tens of thousands of all ages, from tiny tots to the 100+, in poverty stricken villages to plush halls. What a joy to witness their personal transformations. I love inspiring our fellow humans.

My rewards come from the excitement in their eyes, the smiles that fill their faces, and the abundant hugs after each session. My work is my personal journey, and I live a simple life, pouring any revenue back into my volunteer work around the globe.

Now, I share many of the adventurous stories through my writings tinged with fantasy. I'd love for you to explore my books and send me your thoughts and feedback. It's a small world bounding with adventure, and I would love to hear yours.

Lots of love and hugs,

Always,

V.

❋ ❋ ❋ ❋ ❋ ❋

CHARACTERS ON UTOPIAN PLANET ZOOKA

Brela (Jali's Zookian squirrel friend)
Commander ZW1 (Chief of the Peace-Keeping Force)
Elder Lion (Zookian)
Green Tortoise (Zookian)
Guardian 1 (Jali's Teacher)
Jali (Reen'as brother, Queen Vraka's grandson)
Jee (Reena's nick name for Jali)
Mama (Jali's & Reena's mother)
Magnificent ZW7 (Zookian special warriors)
Papa (Jali's & Reena's father)
Peace-Keeping Force (Cosmic Peace Keepers)
Prince Jali (Reena's brother)
Princess Reena (Jali's sister, Queen Vraka's granddaughter)
Protector 1 (Queen Vraka's Advisor)
Queen Vraka (Jali & Reena's Grandma, Queen of Zooka)
Reena (Jali's sister, Queen Vraka's granddaughter)
Tuttles (Jali's Zookian turtle friend)

✳ ✳ ✳ ✳ ✳ ✳

CHARACTERS ON APOCALYPTIC PLANET EARTH

Brelize (Jali's squirrel Earth friend)
Chan (Michael's father, Dragon leader)
Dragons (Chan's evil gang)
First Ones (pure beings)
Herby (doctor, Kriaka's fiance)
Ivan (Dragon)
Kriaka Adi (leader of First Ones)
Kri (Kriaka's pet name)
Meosic (Shiana's cat)
Michael (Chan's son)
Miss Amber (school teacher)
Pierre (supposed follower)
Rama Adi (Kriaka's brother, previous leader of First Ones)
Saks (Dragon)
Shiana (Ana, Kriaka's sister)
Siya (Shiana's friend)
Vincent (Siya's brother)

✳ ✳ ✳ ✳ ✳ ✳

WORLD ON UTOPIAN PLANET ZOOKA

Control Chamber (in Zooble)

Cosmo 13

Cosmos

Field of Detection

Force-1 Shield

Galaxy Al86

Level-4 (Graduation level)

Level-5 (Graduation level)

Lotus Wand (Queen Vraka's ancient spear)

Magical Arrows of Power (Princess Reena's weapons)

Magnificent ZW7 (Zookian special warriors)

Peace-Keeping Force

P1 invisible shield

planet Zooka

Royal Bed

Royal Cave

Royal (Counsel) Chamber

Royal Garden

Royal Guardian

Royal Observation Chamber

Royal Zooble Chamber

Spear of Vee (Princess Reena's weapon)

Summit (hideout to watch Zooble Dome)

Sword of Khadga (Princess Reena's weapon)

Telepathy (communicate via thoughts)

Third Eye (super-conscious powers)

Transporter (to beam over/to cross over)
Utopia (perfect place)
Z-Clock
Z-days
Z-seconds
Zarp-speed
Zooble Dome (lift off deck for space ships)
Zooble intergalactic space explorer-a bubble
Zooka (planet)
Zookian (life-form)
Zookian Glass (hologram communicator)
Zookian Locator (detect intergalactic places)
Zookian-months
Zookish (language on Zooka)

✳ ✳ ✳ ✳ ✳ ✳

WORLD ON APOCALYPTIC PLANET EARTH

Africa (continent)
Arena Park (town in Chatsworth)
Basotho Land (country adjacent South Africa)
Cathedral Peak (mountain area)
Chatsworth (area in Kwa-Zulu Natal)
Draco (Dragon mountain)
Drakensberg (mountain range)
(the) First Ones (Kriaka's pure team)
Giant's Castle (mountain area in Drakensberg)
Gateway (first opening to Portal)
(the) GIFT (mysterious stone)
Jen (bakkie, Rama's truck)
KwaZulu-Natal (eastern province of South Africa)
laanis (rich ones)
Mercedes (fancy car)
Milky Way
Mooi River (town)
Mont Aux Sources (mountain at the source)
planet Earth
Portal
rainbow nation (united in diversity)
South Africa (country on continent of Africa)
Unit 1 (township area in Chatsworth)
Umlazi (Black township)
Zulu (African language)

# # # # # #

DISCOVERING LANGUAGES

abaningi amandla- many powers

aikona-no

amanzi-water

angaz-don't know

ay-hay

bakkie-truck, jeep

bru-bro, fella

Bulnitramet-fantasy element

domkop-idiot

donga-pothole

duffel bag-soft bag

Halloween-horror celebration

Hayibo-wow

jol-party

laanis-rich people

ooka-yes on Zooka

papyrus-paper on Zooka

petrol-gas, gasoline

rainbow nation-unity in diversity

sangoma-tribal doctor

siya bonga-thank you

wungani-how are you

yebo-yes

Zulu-African language

✳ ✳ ✳ ✳ ✳ ✳

My Notes